One

'Look out! Misfit landing!' cried the red-headed boy, who was the first to crash through the front door of number 27 Webb Street, bounce up the hallway, fly across the kitchen and land head first into a sink full of washing-up.

The man sitting at the table eating his breakfast could hardly believe his eyes. He'd just been invaded by a bunch of kids riding giant balloons and wearing fancy dress. He shook his head, closed his eyes, and opened them again. No. He wasn't dreaming, they were still there. In fact, the big one in the tight pink suit was munching on a slice of his toast.

Seymour Potts climbed out of the sink,

5

pulled a soggy piece of paper out of his 'Miskit' box and coughed lightly.

'Good morning. We've come to save you,' he declared, in what he hoped was a confident-sounding voice. 'Now, I understand that a box of cornflakes fell on your head some time this morning and knocked you out.' He stared down at the man and frowned. He didn't look like he'd been knocked out at all. In fact, he looked very well indeed.

'You see,' continued Seymour squinting at his list, 'we're the Magnificent Misfits, the world's newest, toughest fighting force.

And it says here that we save people from mass invasion by alien forces; from flood, fire, hurricanes, and storms of any description; from earthquakes, avalanches and mudslides, runaway trains, bikes and buses, falling trees, falling stars and falling over; and flying objects of any kind, including cereal packets.'

The Magnificent Misfits and the Ghastly Granny

J.J. MURHALL

Illustrated by
Eleanor Taylor

BLOOMSBURY
CHILDREN'S
BOOKS

This book is dedicated to
Michael and Saoirse Ruby,
and to all those 'misfits'
I have ever known,
including the most 'magnificent'
one of all – Alfie.

XX

First published in Great Britain in 1998
Bloomsbury Publishing Plc, 38 Soho Square, London, W1V 5DF

Copyright © Text J. J. Murhall 1998
Copyright © Illustrations Eleanor Taylor 1998

The moral right of the author has been asserted
A CIP catalogue record of this book is available from the
British Library

ISBN 0 7475 3868 9

Printed in England by Clays Ltd, St Ives plc

10 9 8 7 6 5 4 3 2 1

Cover design by Michelle Radford

The
Magnificent Misfits
and the Ghastly
Granny

Ma Vile

Vince Vile

Keith and Timothy Elastic

Barrington Small

Hodge the
Little Horror

Fabian Farquar

Seymour Potts

Elsie Potts
(and Gladys)

He put the piece of paper back in the box and smiled at his fellow Misfits. They didn't look too convinced. But they nodded anyway.

However, before the man could reply, a voice called out from the hallway, and a moment later a young boy hurried into the kitchen. He was about thirteen, had greasy brown wavy hair swept back and loads of

spots. He wore a drab green anorak zipped
tightly up and under his arm he was
carrying a large, fat scrapbook.

'I knew it,' he snorted excitedly. 'I just
happened to be passing and I saw you
crash into the front garden. You're
superheroes, aren't you?'

He stared at Seymour and the others, his
eyes shining eagerly.

'Who are you then? Ninja Lizards? Galaxy boys? You can't possibly be World Warriors, you just don't look brainy enough. A lot of people have never met a superhero before, but I have, see.' And the boy opened his scrapbook to reveal pages of photographs of him standing beside various superheroes. Some of them had been signed and said things like:

To Ninian Soames.
Best wishes Batman.
Or,
Cowabunga! Ninian!

'I can't say that I recognise you lot, though,' said Ninian, narrowing his eyes suspiciously. '*Who* did you say you were?'

'We didn't. But we're the Magnificent Misfits, actually,' replied Fabian Farquar snootily. This was all they needed. A nosy superhero expert quizzing them on their very first day in the job.

'Never heard of you,' replied Ninian, looking disappointed. 'Can you leap over buildings and blow down doors?' He stared at Barrington Small, the biggest of the Misfits.

Barrington shrugged. 'I'm not sure,' he said sheepishly.

'Can you pick up a bus on the end of your finger? Or pull cars along with your teeth?'

'Don't be ridiculous. I'm not a cart-horse,' scoffed Fabian, brushing the front of his spotless white suit distastefully. Fabian Farquar was a very fussy and incredibly clean boy, and he was beginning to think that being a superhero sounded like very dirty work indeed.

Then a small boy called Timothy Elastic peered at Ninian from beneath his enormous hood. 'Listen, mate. This superhero lark isn't all it's cracked up to be, you know. One minute you're just an ordinary school kid, the next, you're running around dressed like an idiot and riding a machine that shouldn't be allowed on the streets. Talk about uncomfortable. My bum feels like it's been clamped in a vice. What's more, we've all been instructed to take this Power Powder stuff every day, and now me and my brother have the power to smell amazingly well, and *that's* no joke either.' He looked at his twin brother Keith, who nodded his head vigorously. Not only were the Elastic twins members of the Magnificent Misfits, they were the Magnificent Moaners as well!

But before the twins could continue, the Misfits' mobile phones began to ring simultaneously, making the most terrible noise. The man at the kitchen table winced and rolled his eyes in exasperation.

'Hello. Elsie Misfit here,' said Elsie Potts, who was Seymour's younger sister. The line crackled and she banged her phone on the table a few times. Then after a moment, a voice came faintly over the line. It was

Omonoslomo, their leader. He was calling from the planet Twart, which was ten thousand light years away.

'Magnificent Misfits, there has been a mistake,' said Omonoslomo with a sigh. He'd had a terrible week. First he'd gone and picked the wrong children to become the world's newest superheroes and now he had a cold coming on. 'Someone has been jamming the airwaves throughout the universe, and giving me the wrong information. No one has been injured by a cereal packet at all. I also heard that a lady has got her head stuck down a rabbit hole somewhere in Slough, and a three-year-old boy is piloting a jumbo jet over the Pacific ocean as we speak. This is all nonsense, of course, and only the Viles could be responsible for this mayhem. They must have landed on earth. Keith and Timothy Misfit, remember to use your super-noses to pick up the smell of extra-strong mints, Vince Vile's favourites. And don't forget, he is a master of disguise, so study everyone that you meet closely. You can bet your life that Ma Vile will be close behind. That granny is as cunning as the fox-fur she wears around her neck, so whatever you do, Magnificent Misfits, keep the object safe. Over and out.'

Seymour and his friends stared blankly at each other. So the Viles had arrived, and

Pickled Onions
May '98

the object that they were after was, of course, the precious jar of pickled onions. Seymour was glad he'd moved it from his sock drawer that morning and put it inside his sister's old toy box. It may look like a harmless jar of onions, but in the wrong hands these pickles were the most powerful weapon in the universe. They could turn children into adults overnight. Kidults, they would be known as, and every child throughout the world would have to work endlessly and never be allowed to play. Even worse, the girls would become their dads, and the boys, their mums!

The man looked up at the Misfits crossly and reached for his spoon.

'Right, if you've quite finished, I'd like to eat my breakfast now,' he said gruffly.

The Magnificent Misfits hastily gathered up their space hoppers and shuffled out of the tiny kitchen. Barrington knocked over a toaster as he went. His space hopper was enormous, ever since he'd mended a puncture and put too much air back in it.

'You'll pay for that!' tutted the man, as Barrington struggled to squeeze through the narrow door-frame.

'And look at those muddy bounce marks you've left on my carpet,' he shouted after them as they hurried up the path, closely followed by Ninian, who watched them intently as they climbed aboard their machines and, after a few false starts, spluttered up into the sky.

Ninian was not convinced. That lot didn't look, or act, like superheroes at all. The Magnificent Misfits needed investigating, and Ninian Soames, superhero expert and all round nosy person, was the only boy for the job.

Two

Changing behind the bike sheds had been a nightmare. The Misfits had squashed their school uniforms into their Miskits that morning, and before school started, they hurriedly put their crumpled clothes on over their costumes. They looked a mess, and Barrington had left his socks and tie at home. But the real problem had been deflating the space hoppers. *That* had taken ages and Elsie had ended up sitting on her Miskit to try and squash it in.

'How come on the telly you never see superheroes going to school?' moaned Keith to his brother during assembly, as they shoved their baggy hoods down the backs of their blazers for the umpteenth time.

However, they did all manage to get through lessons without too much trouble, and Fabian, due to his amazing new eyesight power, was able to see the blackboard quite clearly for the first time all term.

After school, Fabian went home with Barrington because he needed to pick up a library book – on space travel, funnily enough – that his friend had borrowed. Barrington Small lived with his gran and her twenty-five cats in a small and rather smelly house. Fabian didn't like going there very much. However, superhero or not, his book was overdue and he really needed to return it.

As Barrington opened the front door and they stepped into the hall, both boys spotted something straight away. Hanging from the hat stand was a fox-fur, and squatting beside it, buzzing strangely, was

a shopping bag on two sturdy wheels.
Barrington put a finger to his lips as they
tiptoed past it. The fox-fur was snoring
quietly, and from the living room low
voices could be heard.

Suddenly, Barrington's granny called
out, 'Barrington. Is that you? Come in and
say hello to someone.'

Slowly, Barrington pushed open the door
and he and Fabian stepped inside.

His granny was standing by the window facing someone in an armchair who they could not see.

'Ah. There you are, Barrington. Hello, Fabian. Come and meet a long-lost relative of ours,' declared Granny Small delightedly.

The children stepped closer, fearing the worst as the figure in the armchair turned

around to greet them, and they came face to face with *Ma Vile*. She was holding a cup of tea and nibbling on a custard cream. She tried to smile, but it was more like a sneer.

'This is my cousin Flo. Flo Fancy,' announced Barrington's gran. 'She's come from Australia to find me. Isn't it wonderful?'

'Australia, my foot,' muttered Fabian. 'She's from the planet Ghastly and she's conned your granny big-time.'

'I beg your pardon, young man?' called Ma Vile from across the room. 'Being a sweet, shaky old lady, I'm a little hard of hearing. Why don't you come closer?' She stared at the two boys with eyes as cold as ice.

'Yes. Have a nice chat with Flo while I go and make a fresh pot of tea,' said Barrington's granny. And she went off to the kitchen leaving them alone with the ghastly pensioner.

As soon as she had gone, Ma Vile spat

her half-eaten biscuit into her hand and crushed the crumbs into the carpet. Then she threw the remains of her tea into the plant pot that had already begun to wilt beside her, as had the flowers on the mantlepiece. The room was usually bright and sunny, but now this horrible old lady had turned it cold and gloomy.

'Right. Let's cut the small talk,' snapped Ma Vile. 'I know you. And you know me. Just give me those pickled onions and I'll be on my way.' She chuckled to herself hoarsely. 'At least I didn't have to eat that revolting biscuit your stupid granny gave me. Earth food makes me sick. When I take over the world and turn all you kids into Kidults, I'll ban it. And we'll eat Ghastly-type food like boiled sheep's poo or antelope's toenails. Lovely!' She licked her lips hungrily.

'How do you know who we are?' asked Fabian, peering down his nose at her. 'No one's supposed to recognise the

Magnificent Misfits, especially when we're wearing our ordinary clothes.'

Ma Vile cackled. 'Only pea-brained earth beings and my thick-as-a-brick grandson Vince would be fooled by that flimsy disguise. I've never understood why nobody ever recognises that speccy hulk Superman when he's wandering around in a suit and tie. And you-' She indicated towards Barrington. 'You have a label sticking out from under your shirt that says *Made on Planet Twart*.

Ma Vile's eyes narrowed. 'That little girl's playmate fooled me, though. The one that's invisible. Now, that's what I call a disguise. She should come and join forces with me.'

'Find your own pretend friend to play with,' snapped Barrington crossly. Ma Vile was referring to Gladys, Elsie's imaginary friend, and Barrington knew how much she meant to Elsie.

'You rude kid. You'll be the first to go

when I have the Power of the Pickles in my grasp,' hissed Ma Vile, just as Granny Small came back in with the tea tray.

'Have you all been making friends?' she asked brightly.

'Oh yes. We've all been getting along splendidly,' replied Ma Vile, clutching her handbag to her chest and grimacing towards the plant pot. 'But I'm feeling a little tired and being a frail, feeble old lady I'd like to have a lie down now.'

'Of course, Flo. You've come a long way. You must be exhausted,' replied Barrington's granny helping Ma Vile to her feet. 'You can have Barrington's room. He won't mind sleeping on the sofa for a while. Barrington, give Flo a hand with her luggage, there's a good boy.'

Barrington could not believe his ears. His dear, sweet grandma had just invited the most feared old-aged pensioner in the solar system to stay! He and Fabian exchanged anxious looks, both knowing

that they needed to speak to the other
Misfits, and quickly!

'Yes. You'd be *very* surprised at how far
I've travelled today,' replied Ma Vile,
taking hold of Barrington's and Fabian's
arms and leading them into the hallway.
She pulled her beloved Graham from the
hat stand and slung him around her neck.
Then she began to climb the stairs with

Barrington and Fabian following, carrying the shopping cart between them. It weighed a ton and they wondered whatever was in it.

The two Misfits felt helpless and wished that Seymour and the others were there to lend a hand. They'd only been superheroes for a day, and already there was an alien granny invading Barrington's bedroom. It was too much for a kid to take!

The fox-fur opened one beady eye and stared at them over her shoulder. 'Who are they, Mummy?' he growled softly.

'No one special, my little bundle of sugar fluff,' replied Ma Vile, stroking him softly.

When they reached Barrington's room, Ma Vile stopped and held up a skinny hand. 'That's far enough, Misfits. This is *my* room now, and if any of your gang set foot in here, I'll blow this house sky high.' Her eyes narrowed. 'One of you lot has got that jar, and I intend to get it. Mark my word, Magnificent Misfits, this is one granny who *won't* just stay for the week-end smiling sweetly on the sofa. I'm bad, stark raving mad and I'm one mean old lady. *Got it?'* And she stepped inside the room and slammed the door with such force the lampshade on the landing ceiling fell straight on to Barrington's head.

Three

'Speak up, Barrington. I can hardly hear you.' Seymour was soaking in the bath and up to his neck in bubbles. He pressed his mobile phone hard against his ear. His power of hearing had been amazing all day, but now Barrington was barely whispering and he sounded as if he had a box on his head.

'I said, *Ma Vile* is asleep in *my* room. Listen,' hissed Barrington, as Fabian tried desperately to pull the lampshade off.

Barrington put his phone up against his bedroom door, and Seymour heard Ma Vile snoring away like a family of warthogs. The noise was so horrendous, Seymour dropped his phone in the bath

with shock. He fished frantically around
for it, finally retrieving it from the bottom.
It began to froth and bubble from between
the buttons as he put it back to his ear.
Barrington now sounded as if he were
underwater with a box on his head, but
Seymour listened intently as he explained
about who he and Fabian had met that
afternoon in his grandma's living room.

'And is Fabian still with you?' asked Seymour, spitting out bits of foam that he kept sucking up through the mouthpiece.

'Yes. He's trying to get a lampshade off my head,' mumbled Barrington, as Fabian tugged harder.

'OK. See if you can take a peek in Ma Vile's bag while she's asleep,' said Seymour, climbing out of the bath still wearing his Misfit uniform because the zip had got stuck and he couldn't get it off. It seemed to have shrunk a bit more and some of the colour had run. Seymour towelled himself down and rung his hood out in the sink.

'I'll contact the others. We'll be with you as soon as we can. Over and out, fellow Misfits,' said Seymour determinedly.

He ran across the landing to tell his sister, with the feet of his soaking-wet tights slapping against the carpet. Then he rang the Elastic twins, who moaned because they hadn't had their tea yet and they were watching Star Trek. However, he arranged to meet them at six-thirty on the corner of Barrington's street.

'And don't be late,' added Seymour, as he squelched off to get his Miskit and wait for his sister by the garden gate.

Meanwhile, back at Barrington's house, Fabian had finally managed to get the lampshade off his friend's head. Barrington's ears were a bit sore, but he was glad he wouldn't have to walk around wearing it forever. He felt daft enough already.

As quickly as they could, the two Misfits clambered out of their school uniforms and shoved them into the airing cupboard. Then they slowly pushed open the bedroom door. Inside, it was very dark, but through the gloom they could make out the shape of Ma Vile under the duvet, snoring and muttering, with Graham stretched out on the end of the bed and the bag standing as if on guard at the foot of it.

Fabian pushed Barrington in front of him. 'After you,' he whispered politely.

As Barrington stepped forward gingerly, Fabian spotted something shining on the bedside table. It was a glass of water containing Ma Vile's teeth.

'Ugh! Fake teeth,' said Fabian, flaring his nostrils distastefully. 'How positively gross!' He pointed towards the bag. 'Take a look inside,' he urged, pushing Barrington a little further into the room.

'Why me?' asked Barrington crossly.

'Because as well as being super-strong, you've got the power to be incredibly light on your feet,' whispered Fabian. 'And besides, that manky old fox-fur looks like it could do with a good wash, I might catch something off it. Go on, Barrington. Be brave. Take a peep.'

Barrington tutted under his breath and then began to tiptoe across the carpet. The effects of his Power Powder were beginning to wear off and he didn't feel

very nimble at all. He turned and looked at
Fabian who gave him the thumbs up and a
wave. Barrington waved back but just as
he did he trod on something soft and
lumpy.

'SIMON!' he shouted, scooping up his
favourite teddy bear and hugging him to
his chest. 'Did that horrid old granny
throw you on the floor?'

'SSH!' hissed Fabian frantically. But it
was too late, for within the glass Ma Vile's
teeth began to chatter like an alarm
system.

'Yak! Yak! Yak!' they went, splashing
water over the sides. Barrington and
Fabian ran from the room just as Ma Vile
woke and fumbled for the light switch. She
turned it on as they were shutting the door
behind them.

Ma Vile's cold, dark eyes darted around
the room looking into every corner. 'Be
quiet,' she snapped at her teeth. They
stopped immediately and sank to the

bottom of the glass where they lay half open as if they were about to speak.

'Those Misfits have been in here, Graham. I can sense it,' declared Ma Vile, picking the skinny fox-fur up and stroking him. 'I'd better get that machine up and running while you go back to sleep, my little treasure chops.' She began to sing in a voice as rough as sandpaper:

'*Go to sleep. Go to sleep, my sweet little foxy.*
Go to sleep. Go to sleep, your mummy loves
you so.'

Once Ma Vile had tucked Graham in, she
opened up her bag. Inside, it was
enormous. In fact, it was so large it
appeared to have no bottom. Amongst
other things, she fished out a saw, a bag of
nails and various planks of wood. And
then the granny from Ghastly set about
doing a spot of DIY.

Four

Barrington was perched on the window ledge like an overgrown budgerigar. He felt a right fool. People were coming home from work and they kept stopping to look up and point. It was very rude. That was the trouble with being a superhero, people did tend to stare at you a lot. Fabian didn't mind, though. He was standing in the front garden signing autographs like a true celebrity.

Barrington wished Seymour and the others would hurry up. It had been Fabian's bright idea for him to climb up the drainpipe when they'd first heard all the banging and clattering. But now he had, he wasn't too sure what to do next.

Barrington sighed. That was his trouble, he was always being bossed around. Like the time those boys in 5b had made him hand over his dinner money for a whole term, and then got him to steal half a dozen Mars bars from the corner shop. Who was he trying to kid? He wasn't a superhero. He was an overweight clumsy coward in a tight pink suit, stuck on a window ledge and clutching a teddy called Simon.

Barrington was just about to call for help, when from inside the bedroom the banging stopped, and someone down below called up, 'Wow! Your Misfit mate tells me that you really are real live superheroes, and you're going to save the world from a terrible catastrophe. Do you think you can do it?'

Barrington peered down at him. A crowd of people stared back up at him eagerly. He could see that Seymour and the others had landed and were hurrying towards the house. Barrington was feeling a little giddy, but he took a deep breath and smiled. Even if Omonoslomo *had* picked the wrong children, he'd still given them the job. The great ruler of Twart and at least seventeen other planets would be very disappointed if Barrington gave up on his very first day.

'Of course we can!' he announced proudly. 'We're the Magnificent Misfits. We can do *anything*! Nobody messes with us.'

The crowd cheered just as the window was flung open and Barrington went flying off the ledge.

'What's all the racket? Can't a dear, sweet old granny get any peace?' demanded Ma Vile leaning out. Her hair was done up in large plastic curlers, and she was holding a hammer in one hand, and a drill in the other. She looked a gruesome sight, but at least she'd remembered to put her teeth in.

Directly behind her stood a huge teapot-shaped machine which was bubbling and hissing away like a volcano. Ma Vile leant further out of the window and saw Barrington hanging precariously by the back of his suit from the overflow pipe.

'Well, if it isn't old blubber ball himself,' she cackled. 'What are you hanging around for? I thought I told you Misfits to stay away. Now. Either give me those onions or I'll turn on the machine.'

Seymour, who was standing in the front garden, held his Miskit box behind his back. Before he'd had a bath, he'd put the onion jar inside. Somehow he thought it would be safer than Elsie's toy box. Now he wasn't so sure.

'You'll never get your hands on the powerful pickles,' he called up bravely. 'We know all about your plan to make us kids grow up overnight.'

The children in the crowd looked at each other. They didn't like the sound of this very much.

'Right. Then it's time to take action,' said Ma Vile, scowling down at Seymour. 'This machine is called a Spin-Ster and it can make every old lady within a five mile radius fall under my command.' Ma Vile chuckled to herself. 'Grannies of the world are *so* boring. They're just too nice. They like children and flowers and cute little kittens. But above all they love one revolting thing and that's' – here Ma Vile pulled a face like she was about to be sick – 'tea! So I thought I'd invite them round for a cup.' And stepping back, she switched on the machine.

'You leave my granny alone!' shouted Barrington, kicking his legs crossly as the aroma of tea leaves brewing began to waft across the lawn, and a few of the old ladies in the crowd began to twitch and twitter like birds.

Suddenly, without warning, one of them smacked her husband in the face with a carrier bag and then jumped on his foot.

'What did you do that for, Hilda?' cried the man, rubbing his nose and nursing his toe. His wife didn't answer. She was too busy writing HILDA WOZ 'ERE on the garden gate with her lipstick.

Meanwhile, a gaggle of grannies had begun demolishing a phone box, and Barrington's gran, who was returning from

the chip shop, joined in to help. Ma Vile whooped with delight as she watched them emerge from houses, the hairdresser's and the post office, all looking for trouble. They marched up the street stopping only to be extremely rude to some small children, and to chase a poor, defenceless grandad into the park. Ma Vile knew that very soon she would have an army of highly-dangerous old ladies to help her find the precious jar.

Elsie stood at the garden gate holding on to Gladys' hand.

'Behave yourselves!' she shouted loudly, but even her incredible voice power would not deter them, though a couple of people standing beside her leapt back in shock.

'Oh no! There's Mrs Checkocheck,' cried Keith, pointing towards a short, dumpy lady who was pushing a trolley-load of shopping. She proceeded to run someone over with her grocery cart and then crash it into a bus stop. 'She should be at home cooking our tea, not terrorising the neighbourhood,' moaned Timothy, watching in amazement.

Meanwhile, Ma Vile, still with her hair in curlers, and a pint of milk in one hand, had opened the front door and was ushering all the grannies inside.

'Welcome, my naughty, naughty ladies,' she greeted them enticingly, as granny after granny piled into the tiny house. She closed the door behind them.

'I thought you said you were superheroes. A fat lot of good you lot are,' called a familiar voice from the crowd. It was Ninian Soames, still holding his scrapbook and taking notes, as he stood on tiptoe straining to get a better view. A few people mumbled in agreement and began to wander away.

'Looks like we're doomed then, George,' said one man to another.

'I don't know what the world's coming to when a superhero lets you down,' replied his friend, shaking his head.

The Magnificent Misfits looked at each other shamefully. Then Seymour put his Miskit down and hurried over to the front door. 'Actually we've got a plan,' he announced loudly, putting his ear up against the letterbox.

'Have we?' asked Barrington, scratching his head and swinging precariously from side to side. The others looked blankly at each other and shrugged.

'I think Ma Vile's hypnotised them with the smell of some strange tea,' said Seymour, listening intently. 'And now she's making them drink it, 'cause there's an awful lot of slurping going on in there.'

'But Mrs Checkocheck *hates* tea. She only drinks coffee,' declared Timothy huffily. 'So *she* won't have any.'

'Well that's funny,' replied Seymour with a frown, 'because Ma Vile has just asked her if she'd like one lump of sugar or two.'

The Elastic twins looked at each other and gulped. Lovable Mrs Checkocheck had turned into a horrible hooligan. They would be much too scared to moan at her now!

Five

Seymour's plan was simple. Probably
because he'd made it up in about five
seconds flat. They would lie in wait, and
when the grandmas emerged, they would
ambush them.

'I saw a film like that once,' declared
Fabian, ducking down behind a dustbin.
'Only they weren't old ladies, they were
plain clothed detectives.'

'I think I can hear them coming,' said
Seymour, motioning to the crowd to step
back behind the hedge as he and the other
Misfits hid in various places. Seymour put
a finger to his lips and the crowd went
quiet. Everyone held their breath.
Suddenly the front door flew open and all

the grannies came streaming out into the garden. They looked meaner than ever.

Some of them were armed. One held a dustpan and brush as a shield and baton, while Barrington's granny brandished an egg whisk switched on and ready for action. Mrs Checkocheck was wearing a mixing bowl on her head as a helmet, and had slung two washing-up liquid bottles on either side of her belt. She looked like she might reach for them at any moment.

Leading the army was Ma Vile on her rollerblades. She zoomed along igniting sparks on the gravel, with Graham slung recklessly over her shoulder. Suddenly, something caught her eye, and doing a nifty turn she skidded to a halt right in front of Seymour's Miskit box which he'd left on the path.

'Well. What have we here?' declared Ma Vile, bending down and picking it up. Seymour looked fearfully at his sister. Ma Vile opened the box – and took out the

precious pickled onions! They seemed to
vibrate through her fingertips as she
clasped the jar eagerly. Behind her, the
grandmas stood obediently in a long line.

The crowd waited for the Magnificent
Misfits to do something amazing. Seymour
signalled to the Elastic twins.

'BOO!' shouted Timothy, jumping out
from behind a bush and dancing about like
a chicken in a boxing ring. His brother
followed, waving his arms and peering out

from beneath his hood. Ma Vile calmly pulled a huge boomerang-shaped object from her bag. It was almost bigger than she was, but she zapped it between Timothy's toes, making him jump about a foot in the air.

'Ouch! Be careful,' he whimpered. 'You could do some damage with that thing.

'You sissy. I only tickled your toes with it,' chuckled Ma Vile. '*This* is real damage.' And she fired it at a garden gnome, blowing it to smithereens.

'Well. Anything you can do, *we* can do better,' declared Fabian, stepping out from his hiding place and holding his Slapper Blapper in front of him with a flourish. He was a bit uncertain what to do with it because he hadn't read the instructions properly. Fabian wasn't very keen on things that fired and made loud noises. Even a balloon bursting made him want to go and lie down for a week. However, he closed his eyes and fired it anyway.

Unfortunately, he'd been holding it round the wrong way and a moment later his face was covered in a slimy green substance that began to ooze down the front of his spotless white suit.

'Oh no! Just look at the state of me,' he wailed. 'I'll never be able to get these stains out!'

Suddenly, Elsie roared, 'Stick 'em up!' Her booming voice distracted Ma Vile for a

moment. Elsie took her chance, fired her Slapper Blapper and managed a direct hit straight into Mrs Checkocheck's face. As quick as a flash, Mrs Checkocheck reached for her belt and whipped out the two squeezy bottles.

'No, kid. *You* stick 'em up,' she drawled, spinning them between her fingers and squirting them straight at Elsie. Soapy water shot out and soaked the poor girl from head to toe. Then Mrs Checkocheck blew calmly into the tops of the bottles and put them niftily back in her holster belt.

Meanwhile, Ma Vile began to back towards the house, holding the jar with a grip of steel. 'Don't try to follow me or I'll set the grannies on to you,' she declared. 'I'm just going to pick up the rest of my belongings and then I'll be on my way. I've got what I came for. Once I get back to Ghastly, the power of the pickles will be all mine. *Mine*, do you hear me? *Mine! Mine! Mine!*' And she cackled like a woman deranged. But so engrossed was she in sounding like a complete lunatic, that Ma Vile backed straight into the wall of the house and Barrington, who was still dangling directly above, suddenly crashed on to her like a sack of potatoes as his suit finally gave way.

'*Oof!*' went Ma Vile, as the weight of Barrington squashed her.

'*Yowoch!!*' exclaimed Barrington, leaping up as Graham bit him on the bottom.

Ma Vile made a run for it, but Seymour grabbed the washing line and, swinging from it, jumped on to Ma Vile's back. She spun around and around like a whirlwind, with Graham clinging on and turning a rather sickly shade of beige. Suddenly, the manky fox-fur could hold on no longer and he went flying just as Ma Vile managed to shake Seymour off.

'Grannies! Charge!' cried Ma Vile, holding the pickles aloft.

'STOP!' screamed Elsie in her loudest

voice. Everyone turned to face her. In her
hand she held Graham up by the scruff of
his neck. Ma Vile indicated for the
grannies to stop, as the fox-fur struggled to
free himself.

'Let go of me,' he snapped, 'or I'll bite
you.'

'No you won't, you naughty boy,'
replied Elsie, wagging a finger sternly in
front of his nose. 'It's not nice to bite. Learn
some manners.'

Graham stuck his bottom lip out sulkily.

He was used to everyone throughout the universe being scared of him. No one had ever told him off before.

'Give me back my little munchkin,' snapped Ma Vile.

Elsie shook her head. 'We'll do a deal. The fox for the onions.'

'Mummy! Help!' wailed Graham, looking very sorry for himself.

Ma Vile's eyes darted from the jar to Graham and back again. That fox-fur meant everything to her. Perhaps world domination could wait. It wouldn't be the same without Graham as her second in command anyway. She gave the jar one last longing look and then handed it over to Seymour.

'Now give me back my baby,' she snapped angrily.

Elsie shook her head again and everyone gasped. 'Our leader, Omonoslomo, said *never* to trust you,' she replied, picking up her Miskit box and putting Graham inside.

'But if you promise to go back to Ghastly, we'll post Graham on to you.'

Ma Vile glared at Elsie and then at the imaginary Gladys. *Never* had she been cheated on like this, but as Graham was the only thing that she cared about, Ma Vile knew she had no choice.

'Before you go, though, could I have my granny back please,' added Barrington, frowning at Granny Small who looked as if she'd gone into a trance.

'All of these boring old ladies will be back to normal as soon as I've left the planet,' replied Ma Vile, checking her watch. If she hurried she could just catch a ride on a passing satellite and be back on Ghastly by midnight to wait for the post. Just as soon as she had Graham back safely she'd plan her next move. Out there somewhere was her loathsome grandson, Vince. She couldn't possibly let him get his hands on the jar and take over the world. He wouldn't be able to rule the Kidults at all. He was much too thick.

As she reached the garden gate she turned and stared hard at Seymour and the others. 'You've won for now, Magnificent Misfits,' she declared, 'but you'll never stop me. I shall return, and the world and all its kids will be *mine*!' And blowing Graham a kiss she skated off up the road with her shopping bag trailing behind her.

As she whizzed past a battered old ice-cream van that was parked half on the pavement, the driver glanced up. On his lap he had a notepad. Written on it in big scruffy writing was:

Ways to dispose of Grandma
1. Push her down a manhole
2. Send her up in a hot air balloon with a slow puncture
3. Exploding chocolates perhaps?

He screwed up the piece of paper and threw it on the floor. Adjusting his wig, the

man stuffed a handful of extra-strong
mints into his mouth and crunched on
them with his big yellow teeth. Turning
around in his seat, he slid open a partition.

'Lumpy. Gretch. You can come out now,
the coast is clear,' called Vince Vile as the
two little bald-headed figures of his
sidekicks popped their faces over the seat.

''as she gone, boss?' asked one of them
eagerly.

Vince nodded and reached for his sweet
packet. 'They've outwitted her. But they
won't beat me.'

He started his engine and drove slowly past the house. A song called 'If I ruled the world' crackled over the loudspeaker attached to the roof. The Magnificent Misfits who were now surrounded by adoring grandmas, as well as Ninian Soames who still nosing around, looked over. As the van cruised slowly past, the Elastic twins sniffed the air.

'I can smell mints,' remarked Timothy.

'Me too,' said Keith.

Fabian stared hard at the van which was now some distance away. The number plate read:

0 VILE 1

Fabian frowned and thought hard for a moment. And then *not* putting two and two together, he shrugged and happily took off on his space hopper in the direction of the launderette. Maybe the number plate connection would come to him when he was watching the tumble dryer going around and around.

'My grandson Barrington will be so sorry that he missed you,' said Granny Small who was back to being a sweet rosy-faced old lady again. She pinched Barrington's cheek fondly. 'I don't know where he's got to. But there's a *wooden* teapot in his bedroom, which is very strange.'

Barrington smiled at her and said nothing. He couldn't believe she didn't recognise him in his Misfit suit. Omonoslomo had been right.

A moment later the leader of seventeen planets called. 'Congratulations, Magnificent Misfits. You have beaten Ma Vile.' Seymour and his friends grinned at each other, while Ninian Soames looked on enviously. Perhaps he'd been wrong about these so-called superheroes – he'd better get their autographs just in case.

'But remember Misfits,' continued

Omonoslomo, his voice crackling loudly over the phone, 'your work is not yet over. Vince Vile is out there somewhere. You must keep those pickled onions safe at all costs. Find another place to hide them. Keep your eyes peeled and your lips sealed and your hands upon your onions, because the world depends on a Misfit. Keep taking the Power Powder. Over and out, Magnificent Misfits.'

*

The next day at school, the only game being played in the playground was one called 'The Magnificent Misfits'.

Everyone wanted to be a Misfit, and there were plenty of arguments about who should be who.

Seymour and his friends leant against the wall and watched silently. As usual, nobody asked them to join in but had just remarked:

'You're too weird,' or

'No way, fatty,' and

'You talk too posh.'

But today they didn't mind. They clutched their Miskits tightly and remembered just who they *really* were.